The ROYAL SWITCH

The ROYAL SWITCH

The Duchess of York

A YEARLING BOOK

Published by
Bantam Doubleday Dell Books for Young Readers
a division of
Bantam Doubleday Dell Publishing Group, Inc.
1540 Broadway
New York, New York 10036

ISBN: 0-440-41213-7

American English has been used throughout this book.

Reprinted by arrangement with Delacorte Press

Printed in the United States of America

November 1997

10 9 8 7 6 5 4 3 2 1

CWO

To my best friends,
Beatrice and Eugenie

Dear Reader,

I am delighted that you are about to read my newest book projects—two companion novels about the delightful escapades of an adventurous princess and her look-alike friend.

The Royal Switch and *Bright Lights* are novels about Princess Amanda, a mischievous redheaded girl who lives in an elegant world—a world into which I have special insight—and her desire to break free from its constraints. Her friend, an American eleven-year-old named Emily, who is *not* a princess, understands how it feels to face disappointments and then to bounce back and seek good times again.

It is my hope that this energetic pair's engaging adventures, set against the colorful backdrop of two dynamic cities—London and New York—will win your heart.

As the mother of two young princesses, I know the importance of reading and sharing books. I remember how much I loved to be drawn into books that swept me away to enchanting places and took me on exciting adventures. It is thrilling to be able to write stories that can be read not only by my own girls, but also by wonderful young girls all over the world, girls like you.

I hope you will have as much fun reading *The Royal Switch* and its companion, *Bright Lights,* as I had creating the stories for you.

Sincerely,

Sarah, The Duchess of York

The ROYAL
SWITCH

Chapter One

It was early morning, and in Amanda's dream the cloudless sky was an exquisite blue, when suddenly a flash of pink zoomed upward. Amanda's mummy and daddy had taken her for a hot-air balloon ride. There were no fax machines, no telephones, no guards along. Her daddy did have a beeper—just in case of an emergency—but he promised not to use it unless he absolutely had to.

At first they soared over their own land. The palace and gardens looked splendid. The balloon continued to float but changed direction and smoothly headed toward the forest. They looked down on the parish church,

1

where the great abbey had once stood. There was no one else in the gondola of the balloon—just Mummy and Daddy and herself, Amanda. Even in her sleep, that made her smile, because having her parents all to herself was something that hardly ever happened.

As Amanda rolled onto her left side in the bed, the scenery in her dream changed. Now the balloon hovered over the wild landscape that was the Highlands of Scotland, and she listened as her father's voice spun stories about the tragic feuds that had raged there long ago.

The dream balloon swayed to the left, and Amanda began to feel uncomfortable. When it began to shake, Amanda was thrown from one side of the gondola to the other. She opened her mouth to scream, but nothing would come out. Mummy and Daddy were still visible to her, but they didn't seem to see that Amanda's feet were caught in some ropes or netting on the floor of the balloon. Amanda wriggled her legs back and forth, but she couldn't dislodge the netting no matter how hard she tried.

Suddenly she sat up in bed with her round blue eyes opened wide.

The dream evaporated, its details forgotten, but something was moving against her legs. Amanda, now awake, lifted the soft eiderdown and peered underneath it. Now she was able to scream, and she did!

"Amanda! Oh, my, what is it, what's happened?" Nanny appeared instantly. She bent over Amanda, frowning with concern.

Amanda had leapt out of the bed and was pointing to the pink sheets with a jabbing forefinger.

"Look! Look, Nanny, look at that!"

"I say!" Nanny put her hand to her chest. "It's a—toad, isn't it?"

Amanda's face was as red as her hair. She put her hands on her hips. "It's a frog,

Nanny, it's a frog, that's what it is. And do you know who put it there? In the middle of my bed?"

"Ribbit," the frog croaked, and looked around, apparently unconcerned that he was sitting atop an embroidered crest on fine linen sheets.

Nanny jumped back as she anxiously said, "I'll call Bess," and then pulled on a velvet rope.

"Do you know how this frog got here?" Amanda demanded.

"Why, I—"

"I do! I know!" Amanda cried. She could smell the faint odor of lavender water coming from the gray cardigan Nanny wore over her blue uniform. "It was George! It was Cousin George!"

"Amanda!" Nanny cried, shocked. "He's a fine young lad!"

"George doesn't treat me properly. He's angry at me because I'm not going to his birthday party this afternoon. This frog in my bed is his way of paying me back! Oooooh!" She narrowed her eyes and stamped her foot. "Sometimes he just makes me so—so—Oooooh!"

A maid knocked and appeared in the doorway of Amanda's bedroom. She looked questioningly at Nanny, who simply pointed to the frog, which was still on the sheets in spite of Amanda's shrieks.

"Ribbit," the frog repeated.

"Take it away," Nanny said, waving at the maid, who gingerly untied her apron and scooped up the frog.

"I'll bring it to the gardener," the maid managed to say, and left.

Nanny turned to Amanda, whose hand was over her mouth to suppress her laughter.

"Did you see Bess's face?" Amanda giggled. "She looked as if you'd asked her to do a dance on Daddy's dinner table. She really did a smashing job using her apron to get it out of here."

Nanny had recovered by this time. "You're lagging behind this morning, Princess Amanda," she said.

"Yes, you're right, Nanny," Amanda answered brightly. Nothing was going to spoil this day for her. She had looked forward to it for weeks.

"Go dress and clean your teeth," Nanny instructed. "I've laid out your clothes."

Amanda glanced at the dark green corduroy shorts and pale green shirt, her knickers and vest, her ankle socks and her stiff, polished brown lace-ups standing next to each other on the floor under the chair.

"Thank you, Nanny," she said dutifully. Actually, she hated the clothes, but today she was happy to wear them for a chance to spend the day with her parents.

As she went to wash up, Amanda began to

sing. It was her habit to start her morning with a song. Nanny always looked forward to it, although she never said a word to her charge. The child had a lovely voice, but Nanny didn't want to swell her head.

This morning Amanda was humming "Greensleeves." At times the tune seemed to have a bit of a mournful quality—somewhat like the child herself. . . .

My, Nanny thought, soon she won't be a child anymore. She certainly is getting big!

Amanda was of average height for her ten and a half years, but to Nanny, who had spent most of her life taking care of babies, Amanda was becoming quite a handful.

Babies! Nanny pursed her lips and shook her head. They were easier, certainly, and they didn't have minds of their own yet. But the trouble was, when a baby grew out of that toddler stage, someone else took over and you had to change jobs, move on, settle in with another family, another baby. You never got to sleep a whole night through!

"Amanda?"

"Yes, Nanny, I'll be right there. . . ."

So now Nanny was watching young Princess Amanda grow, practically before her eyes. It was an interesting experience, to say the least.

"It probably was her cousin George," Nanny said to herself, and reached for the intercom to call down to the kitchens for their breakfast to be brought up.

They sat opposite each other in the nursery, as they did every morning. Amanda stared off into space, a tiny, playful smile on her lips.

"It's a lovely boiled egg." Nanny spooned up her own while she gestured to Amanda with her other hand. "Come now, let's eat it while it's hot."

"Nanny, did you know Queen Victoria had nine children?"

"Amanda." Nanny waved her fingers at the strips of toasted brown bread. "Dip your soldiers in that egg, now."

"Nine children!" Amanda said. "Do you suppose each one of them had a nanny of his or her own?"

"Amanda—"

"Or was there just one nanny? For all of them. Or maybe there were two or three. Perhaps for the younger children . . ."

"Amanda, you've hardly touched your porridge." Nanny patted the corners of her mouth with her linen napkin.

"I must remember to look that up," Amanda mused. She sipped her milk from a delicate, square china cup.

Nanny thought again about all the babies she had tended, and she sighed as she neatly folded her napkin and placed it next to her plate. Babies don't speak to you or ask you

10

questions you can't answer or challenge you in any way. All you have to do is keep their tummies full and see that they burp and that their nappies get changed.

Nanny sighed. She watched Amanda's profile as the Princess stared out the window at the gardens below. Where on earth did the child get hair that color? As red and shining as a sunset in August! Her mother had dark hair, almost black, and her daddy's was a deep brown, too. None of her cousins had red hair, either. Well, little Lady Catherine's was a sort of strawberry blond, but nothing like this! It was beautiful, Nanny thought, and she did love brushing it each night before Amanda's bedtime—a hundred strokes. Sometimes they counted together.

Those freckles, though. Try as Nanny might to keep the child out of the sun, to make sure she had on a broad-brimmed hat, especially in spring and summer, still, some-how, that sun managed to get through and dot-dot-dot Amanda's arms, legs, chin, cheeks!

"Amanda?"

"Hmm?" Amanda was still smiling at the gardens.

"Amanda!"

Now she swiveled around. "Yes, Nanny?" A finger pointed to a sliver of toast, and Amanda picked it up and ate it reluctantly.

"Your mother expects to see you as soon as she's had her breakfast," Nanny said.

Amanda clapped her hands. "I know, I know! We're to plan our day together! Remember? Today's the day Mummy and Daddy promised to spend with me! Just the three of us! And I get to choose some of the things we'll do." In her excitement, Amanda wiggled around in her chair. Nanny frowned, but only slightly.

"I thought we could take a picnic hamper! And that we could eat outdoors under the willow tree near the duck pond! And we could talk and make up stories and play games, and then we could take a ride over to— Oh!"

"You've tipped your cup," Nanny said, moving quickly to wipe up Amanda's milk with her napkin. Then she stood. "We had better see if your mother is ready for you."

Amanda's mother, the Princess of Powers Court, was at her desk in her sitting room arranging papers when her daughter entered.

"Good morning, Mummy." Amanda kissed her mother on both cheeks.

"Good morning, Amanda." Her mother smiled. She smelled wonderful, not like lavender water or Brussels sprouts, the way Nanny always smelled. Amanda loved the scent her mother wore.

"Mummy." Amanda was careful to keep her voice calm. "I've been so looking forward to today!"

"Yes, I, too, darling, but I'm afraid your

daddy and I must fly to Scotland this morning." She tucked her papers into an open drawer of her desk and slid it shut. Then she looked up at Amanda. "I'm so sorry, my sweet."

Amanda bit down hard on her lower lip.

"But"—her mother took Amanda's two hands in her own and smiled her special smile—"you won't have much time to be disappointed. There's something much more fun for you to do today."

Amanda frowned and tilted her head.

"Don't you remember? Today is Cousin George's birthday party!"

Amanda swallowed hard and clamped her teeth together.

"Yes, of course you remember!" her mother went on. "Haven't you told me how he always teases you about being so much younger than he, when there's only four months' difference between you! Well!" Her mother stood, and Amanda backed up

14

slightly. "Now you'll be able to go to the party after all! I'm sure you're pleased about that, now aren't you?"

Amanda's stomach lurched, but she bit down harder on her lip and continued to look up at her mother.

"We'll have our lovely day together sometime soon, dear," the Princess said, "when we get back. Meanwhile, you run along with Nanny and decide which lovely frock you'll wear this afternoon."

"Yes, Mummy," Amanda whispered. As much as she wished she could cry and beg, she held herself straight and turned to go back to her rooms.

"I don't want to go to horrible Cousin George's party!" she said through clenched teeth as she and Nanny walked along the corridor. "And after this morning—that frog! How did Cousin George get into my bedroom without someone seeing him? Not that he'd ever tell me. . . ."

Nanny walked briskly. Amanda's golden-red hair bounced as she hurried along.

Nanny looked down at the sunset-colored hair. She was sad to see that Amanda had been badly disappointed.

"It was supposed to be our day together!" Amanda said sharply.

"You are special, keep that in mind! You've been born into a special world. Come along. Smile and be cheerful. I'm certain your parents will keep the promise they've made as soon as they can arrange it."

Amanda pulled herself up to her full height and straightened her shoulders. Her eyes were shining, but she blinked back any sign of tears. She took a deep breath.

"Yes, Nanny," she said softly. She realized that it was better to hide bad thoughts and hurt feelings; then no one would know she wanted to cry. It could be her secret. She could pretend she was happy.

Nanny looked away, relieved. She hated to see Amanda cry.

Back in her bedroom, alone for a moment, Amanda allowed herself another fit of anger.

"A frog in my bed!" she muttered to herself. "No special day with Mummy and Daddy! And now I have to go to stupid, awful Cousin George's party after all! Ooooo!" She growled.

Amanda reached for her favorite toy, a plush stuffed monkey, which was almost crushed between the feather pillows on her bed. "I'll see you tonight, Mr. Squeaks," she said, kissing the monkey on the nose. When she was very small, she had seen a real monkey—brought by an entertainer to a party—and everyone had made a huge fuss over it. There had been a terrible lot of people at the party. The monkey had squealed and squeaked, and Amanda had thought it must be frightened. Even though the people had been excited and friendly, how could the poor monkey be sure of what was happening? So Amanda tried to make her monkey, Mr. Squeaks, feel loved and safe.

She glanced over at her CD player on its shelf. Music always made Amanda feel better when she was angry or blue. The small, square CD package on top of the player brought a smile to her face. She went over and picked it up. Four male faces with long-ish brown hair grinned up at her from the cover.

"The Mashed Potatoes!" Amanda said out loud, grinning back at them. "I love them so much! They are so cute!"

Amanda loved music. She was familiar with Italian and German opera; she enjoyed show tunes, folk tunes, pop, and rock and roll equally. It depended on her mood.

Now she was in the mood for her favorite new group, which was taking London by storm—the Mashed Potatoes. But as she lifted the CD cover, her shoulders slumped again.

They're giving a concert soon, she remembered. The Mashed Potatoes will be giving a concert and I won't be there! We can get tickets to anything in the whole world we want to see and I won't be there for the next Mashed Potatoes concert. She mimicked Nanny's prim voice: " 'Princess A-*man*-da at a rock concert? I do not think so!' "

That's what they'd say, Amanda thought with a sigh. All of them. I can have all the CDs I choose, but I must not show how undignified I am by going to a rock concert! Now that's four beastly things: Frog-in-bed! No special day with Mummy and Daddy! Beastly Cousin George's party! And now, no Mashed Potatoes concert to look forward to!

Amanda glanced at the party clothes laid out before her.

"Pink is lovely on you, Amanda, with your gorgeous hair," Nanny said, smoothing the folds of the frock. It was similar to many party frocks Amanda had, with smocking in front, puffed sleeves, and white pearl buttons. The white cardigan had pearl buttons, too.

But the petticoat itches awfully, Amanda thought, looking at the stiff, pale pink crinoline on its hanger. And the tights will be hot. . . .

"Come now, let's get ready. How very sweet you're going to look. See how shiny those black patent leather shoes are! And how shall we do your hair?"

This isn't at all the way I planned this day, Amanda grumped.

Chapter Two

The elegantly appointed hotel room was a mess! Clothes were strewn on the furniture; an old rag doll with red yarn hair was draped over a lampshade, arms and legs dangling; a laptop computer sat open on a corner desk, under which a wastebasket overflowed with crumpled papers. The telephone was hidden under a wet towel on the desk, and its muffled double rings brought Emily running from the bathroom as her parents came through the door.

"Emily Jane Chornak!" her mother began. "Look at this place—"

"Wait." Emily held up her hand as she

spoke into the phone. "Hello?" She listened a moment and sighed. "It's for you," she told her father, and held the receiver out to him. He stepped over jeans and a baseball cap and took the telephone.

Her mother grinned at her. "Did you think it would be for you, Em?" she asked. "I know you and Stacy promised to keep in touch over spring vacation, but I don't think she's calling from her bike trip."

Emily tried not to roll her eyes. "Sure, I guess I did. Just like home."

"Mmm-hmm. Just like home." Emily's mother looked around. "And just like home, this place is a mess already. Start picking some of these things up, young lady. It's all your stuff."

"Not the papers! Not the computer! That's yours and Dad's!"

"Right. You clean up the rest and we'll see how much computer mess there really is."

As Emily grabbed the rag doll, the jeans,

and the baseball cap, she turned to look back at her mother. "What are we going to see first?" she asked. "The Tower of London? Madame Tussaud's wax museum? Can we see the Tower of London first? Please, Mom? Mrs. Wright says two queens got their heads cut off there! I promised Stacy I'd send her plenty of postcards, and I want to get started."

"Emily, really. There are wonderful sights to see all over London and that's your first choice? The Bloody Tower?"

"Right!" Emily said, and rubbed her hands together.

Emily's father hung up the phone. "That was Edward Clarin," he said, addressing Emily's mother. "He's arranged for us to meet his client, but it must be at his flat at one."

Emily frowned and looked from one parent to the other. "At *one*? But that wrecks the whole day! We were supposed to spend the day together and see all the sights! You promised! Can't he change the time? What's the big deal?"

"Emily, do you know why we're here? Why we came to England?"

"I guess so. . . ."

"It's a business trip, honey. We wanted to bring you, of course, but it's still an important business trip. We have to get these people to sign with us. It's very important."

"I know, but—"

"Look," Emily's mother said, glancing at her watch. "It's only nine-thirty and none of us has eaten yet. Why don't you get dressed, sweetie, and we'll take you downstairs, have a little breakfast, and decide what we'll do. Okay?"

"Some croissants, black coffee, maybe some oatmeal—uh, porridge, for my daughter." Emily's mother was looking up from the breakfast table, talking to the waiter.

"It's not fair," Emily said grumpily. "We

24

were going to see all the sights. Now I'll be stuck here all day watching TV. And I don't even like these programs."

"Emily, please. We'll find something for you to do," her father said. "We'll think of something."

"Something . . ." Emily poked at the silverware.

"My, what lovely red hair your daughter has," the headwaiter said brightly, peering at Emily as he stopped by their table.

Emily's mother smiled. "She does, doesn't she? It's my mother's color, that copper red."

"Very unusual."

"Everyone says that, don't they, Emily?"

Emily rolled her eyes, but no one saw because she had turned her head to look out the window.

"She's upset because we were all supposed to go sightseeing together," Emily's mother explained. "But now it seems our appointment has been moved up to one o'clock, and we won't be able to take Emily on the tour we promised."

"I beg your pardon, but if you'll speak to the concierge, he'll have just the thing. There's a children's tour of London that leaves from right outside the hotel—right there!" The headwaiter pointed to the revolving doors. "That's where the tour leaves from. That red kiosk across the street every weekday morning at ten-forty-five sharp! It's for children between eight and twelve. No adults."

"Really?" Emily's mother's face lit up.

"Puh-leeze." Emily groaned. She couldn't believe her parents were embarrassing her in front of the waiter.

"Give it a chance, Em," her father said, gulping a cup of coffee. "At least let's find out about it." Emily followed her parents to the concierge's desk.

"Yes, there's a minibus that picks the children up at their various hotels. Quite conve-

nient, what?" the curly-haired man at the desk said. "It's a blue minibus. It says 'London Tours for Children.' The first stop is the Changing of the Guard at Buckingham Palace. That starts at half past eleven, but you want to be there early because of the crowds."

"And how long is the tour?" Emily's father asked.

"It's approximately four and a half hours, with a stop for lunch. It leaves the children off at Victoria Station, and parents can collect them there."

"Perfect!" Emily's mother said. "If we're meeting Edward and the group at one and Emily's tour ends up at Victoria Station at—what, three-fifteen?—why, that gives us plenty of time to finish everything up!"

Emily kept her head down, but her eyes moved from her mother to her father as if watching a tennis match.

"Perfect!" Emily's father echoed. "Then it's settled!"

"Well, swell," Emily said finally. "I'm glad *you* two are happy."

Her parents looked down at her.

"Emily, this solves everything," her mother said. "You get to see London, and we get to have our business appointment. We'll all meet later and have a nice supper and see a play or hear a concert. If this works out, we'll have a wonderful surprise for you."

"But I wanted to see London with you," Emily said, twisting her fingers together. "You promised me at least one day. . . . You did, you promised! You *never* keep promises—"

"It's a lovely tour," the concierge interrupted, nodding from behind the desk. "Truly, it is, you'll see. Why don't you run up and put on something pretty—you understand, a frock or something. You'll be meeting some fine young people, to be sure."

Back in their rooms, Emily said with a fake English accent, " 'Why don't you run up

29

and put on something pretty!' " She wrinkled her nose. "What the heck's wrong with what I have on right now?"

They stood in the middle of the room. Emily's mother, fist pressed to her chin, eyed the clothes in Emily's wardrobe.

"What's wrong with it?" Emily persisted.

"Obviously, jeans and yellow tube tops are not what they wear on London-for-children tours," her mother said. "I think that's what the concierge was trying to tell us. What can we— Ahhh!" She pulled out a pink dress, still in the dry cleaner's plastic bag. "This'll be great!"

"Mo-ther!" Emily cried.

"What?"

"It's a little kid's dress! It has puffy sleeves, for Pete's sake! I didn't even know you packed that!"

"It's not a little kid's dress. You wore it just two months ago to your school concert. It's beautiful on you. You'll look like what you are—an eleven-year-old girl—instead of like the punk rockers your father and I represent. That's between us, of course." Her mother smiled at her own remark.

"Do I have to?" Emily asked.

"You do! And these."

"White tights? And black Mary Janes? Come on, Mom! That's *disgusting*."

But her mother was firm. "These are very light. They're really stockings, Emily. And the shoes top off the outfit. You mustn't forget, you are in another country. You want to put your best foot forward. It doesn't matter what the other children wear. You're representing the United States now."

"Oh, sure . . . I'm the ambassador. From Brooklyn Heights."

The telephone rang, and Emily's father picked it up.

"Forget it, Em, you're not wearing jeans," Emily's mother said.

Emily's father put down the phone and looked at his wife. "Edward wants to meet with us *before* we see and hear you-know-who," he said. "He wants to go over our plan to make sure it all runs smoothly at the meeting."

Emily's mother made an exasperated sound. "Oh, well, I suppose that makes sense," she said. "When does he want to meet?"

"Now," Emily's father answered.

"Now?" Emily wailed. "We can't even have *any* time together? And anyway, who is 'you-know-who'? Is there something going on I don't know about?"

Emily's father sat down on the bed so that his eyes were level with his daughter's. Then he put his hands on her shoulders.

"Em, this is a big deal for us. The agency is branching out. We've come over here to meet and try to represent this new—ah, talent."

"Sure."

"So this is very important. Not that you're not."

"Right."

"But after all, that's why we're here. Okay?"

"Okay, but this always happens," Emily said. "Every time we make any plans there's always something that comes up, another concert, an important performance, and you guys have to go on some kind of trip."

"Not always."

Always, Emily thought, deciding not to say anything more.

"Well. Doesn't Emily look lovely?" her mother said, smiling.

"Adorable. My little princess," her father said, and kissed the top of her head.

Emily made her lips purse. *Adorable.* Swell.

They stopped at a little store in front of the kiosk and bought Emily two cookies, which the woman at the counter called biscuits, and a container of milk to go.

"Now, remember, Emily, at ten-thirty you come out of the hotel and stand right here. The concierge will remind you. I hate to leave you now, but it's not too long until you'll be going. It's a minibus. Blue, I think he said. And it says—"

"'London Tours for Children,' I know," Emily told them.

"Yes. And the first stop is—"

"The Changing of the Guard at Buckingham Palace," Emily intoned. "It starts at eleven-thirty, but we have to get there early to beat the crowd."

"Em, there are a lot of people in the world who never get to see anything like this," her mother scolded.

Emily nodded, contrite. "I know," she said. "I want to see all this stuff, honest. It's just that I wanted us to do it together. It's no fun doing everything by myself."

Emily's mother patted her on the head.

"We'll do things together soon. I promise.

And you won't be by yourself today—you'll be able to make some great new friends."

"Sure, Mom."

"Do you have your jacket?"

Emily held it up.

"A jeans jacket, Em? It doesn't really go—"

"It goes fine! And my wallet will fit in the zip-pocket. I really don't think I want to do this. . . ."

"You'll have a wonderful time," her mother said.

"I'm sure you'll meet a lot of very interesting people," her father said.

This isn't what I thought this day would be like, Emily grumped.

Chapter Three

"This looks horrid, and I don't want to go," Amanda said softly to herself as she stared into the full-length mirror. But Nanny's sharp ears picked up her words anyway.

"Fasten those shoes and stand up straight! It's almost time to go."

Amanda obeyed and then examined herself again in the glass. Out of the corner of her eye, she saw Nanny rummaging around in her cardigan pocket for the mints she always nibbled. Amanda used the opportunity to stick out her tongue at Nanny's reflection. "I'm a princess, after all," she said.

"Exactly!" Nanny concurred with a stiff nod, missing Amanda's point. "And a beautiful one, too. Pink is so lovely on you, Amanda." Nanny stepped back and admired her charge. Children today are just young whippersnappers, she thought. None of them is as well behaved or as bright and attractive as my Amanda. "Now, let's hurry—your cousin George will be missing you." She handed Amanda an elegantly wrapped birthday present. Amanda didn't even ask what was inside.

Cousin George, if he misses me at all, Amanda thought, will be wanting someone to tease and annoy. This is going to be just dreadful. And I should have been out with Mummy and Daddy. . . .

She and Nanny walked together through the long corridors.

"There's to be a magician," Nanny said. "You've always loved magic tricks, haven't you, Amanda? Pulling white doves from tall hats, colored scarves from sleeves, making objects disappear . . ."

I wish someone could make me disappear, Amanda thought, but aloud she answered, "Yes, Nanny." There's always a magician, she thought. Or a clown. But the clown performs magic tricks, so I guess it's the same thing.

Oh—except for the time the entertainer brought a monkey! She smiled to herself. That's where I first saw a real one. At a party—Cousin Catherine's! And that's when I wanted a monkey of my own.

Of course, she couldn't have a real monkey—not to keep in her room, anyway—but Mr. Squeaks was almost as good. She decided that if she couldn't spend the day with her parents, she would like to spend it in her room. Perhaps she and Mr. Squeaks could watch something on the telly.

An elevator, then another long corridor.

"It won't be long until your own eleventh birthday, Amanda," Nanny was saying. "We'll have to think about how to celebrate."

A party, Amanda thought with a sigh, with a magician. Balloons, the table with the food laid out in the center, everything looking exactly as it will at Cousin George's party. And many of the same children will be there, too.

"Here we are!" Nanny cried happily as she urged Amanda forward with a two-fingered touch on her shoulder.

"This is a focused tour, as you can understand," the guide was saying as she stood at the front of the minibus. She held a small microphone, even though she didn't really need one. Emily had counted twelve children including herself: seven girls and five boys. None of the girls was wearing jeans, although most of the boys were. Two girls who seemed to know each other well were wearing shorts. They would be the only comfortable ones on the trip, Emily thought. She stuffed her arms into the sleeves of her jeans jacket. Even though some girls were wearing skirts, her pink dress stood out in her mind as childish and too dressy. And Mary Janes! Geez, Mom!

"Our first stop, as you probably know from reading your pamphlets, is Buckingham Palace, where we will watch the Changing of the Guard. Buckingham Palace is the official residence of the Queen. You'll be interested to know that you can tell whether or not Her Majesty is at home by whether the Royal Standard is flying at the masthead."

Who are you, anyway? Emily thought as she half listened to the guide. As you probably know, you are a bore.

Emily had a window seat and was now

gazing out at the street. They drive on the wrong side here, she remembered. Somebody's probably going to get in an accident or something.

"Buckingham Palace was built of red brick as a country house for the Duke of Buckingham. In 1762 it was bought by King George the Third, who needed room for his fifteen children," the guide was saying.

Sure, I guess you need a palace for fifteen children, Emily thought. When do we get to the Tower of London?

"You must be boiling in those stockings! How come you're wearing them?"

Emily turned quickly to find the girl in the seat next to her staring down at her legs.

"Excuse me?"

"I mean, aren't you hot? *I'm* hot just in this denim skirt and I don't even have socks on! Oh! Maybe you're a foreigner! Sorry." And then the girl began to speak more loudly, with pauses between her words.

42

"Do—you—speak—English?" she yelled in Emily's face.

Emily looked the girl up and down and decided that she didn't like her.

"I *am* a foreigner," she replied. "I'm American."

The girl blushed. "Oh, well, but you know what I mean. I'm American, too. I'm from Detroit."

Emily looked at her.

"Michigan," the girl explained.

Emily exhaled loudly. "I know where it is," she answered.

"So what's your name, Red? I bet it doesn't even matter what your name is 'cause everyone calls you Red, right?"

She was grinning. Emily swallowed hard.

"You have that great red hair and that's what you get stuck with. My name's Debbie."

Debbie had a full, round face topped off

with a thick fringe of brown bangs pushed to the side. It was obvious that without constant pushing, Debbie's bangs would hang nearly down to her eyes. She also had round shoulders, round arms, and a round body. She peered at Emily through fancy sunglasses.

"See those two girls across the aisle from us?" Debbie lowered her voice but rudely pointed at them. "They're from France. They know each other from home. When they speak English, they sound so funny. They can't get the sound *th*—you know. I met them on a tour yesterday. They don't speak to anyone anyway, so it doesn't matter. I think they're stuck-up."

Emily turned in her seat to watch a big red double-decker bus pass by.

"We went on a different tour," Debbie said. "It was so cool!"

Emily stared out the window, and Debbie stopped talking for a second.

"So how come you're wearing stockings,

anyway?" Debbie repeated. "I bet your mother made you!"

⁂

"I'm going to leave you for a little while, Amanda," Nanny said, fluffing up Amanda's pink puffed sleeve.

"I'm fine, Nanny," Amanda said.

"Yes, you'll be quite all right. There are all these children here, your cousin, and Jack"— she nodded toward the security man and chauffeur who stood at the door—"will be looking out for you while I'm gone."

"There's my cousin Amanda!" a shrill boy's voice called out. Amanda winced. "It's a grand party, isn't it? I'm eleven now, you know."

Amanda took a deep breath and prepared to face her cousin George. She knew just what he'd be wearing—gray flannel trousers, a navy blazer, a white shirt, and a tie with the family crest on it. She wondered if he knew she had come to the party only because her parents had disappointed her. No matter. She had to make do. Amanda pushed the wrapped present toward Cousin George.

"It's the lovely *frog* you put in my bed this morning! Pull on its leg and it will sing 'Happy Birthday to You'!" Amanda stuck out her tongue at him.

George laughed but didn't apologize. "You picked an outing with your parents over my party," he told her. "I thought you deserved something for that. Besides, it's not a frog I want to sing for me. That's *your* job, my songbird cousin!"

"As the Americans say on the telly, in your dreams, Cousin George!"

"So I'm eleven now," Cousin George persisted. He was grinning at her. He was glad she had been able to come to his party. He really *had* been disappointed when he'd heard she had chosen not to attend. Amanda was always thinking of splendid things to do, and she never seemed to be afraid of anything. He remembered the time she'd jumped into the fountain in the garden—in the middle of a garden party!

She gazed around the room. Mostly boys, she noted as the guests milled about. Boring. She looked for Nanny but then remembered Nanny had gone to do something and couldn't rescue her. Amanda couldn't believe Cousin George was genuinely glad she was there. She turned her attention back to him.

"I *know* you're eleven now, Cousin George," she said with a sigh.

"And you're still only ten," Cousin George added with a laugh in his voice.

"I'll *be* eleven in four months," Amanda said, exasperated.

Cousin George wished she'd get into the

spirit of his teasing. "Look at all the lovely treats, Amanda. We'll have a jolly good time today. *Especially* when you sing!"

—␍␍—

"How long do we have to wait here?" a tall boy named Roy asked as he leaned against the wrought-iron railing in front of Buckingham Palace. "It's hot."

"About twenty-five minutes or a half hour," the guide, Fiona Halles, answered politely. "We always arrange to arrive here early to get a front location. You wouldn't see anything very well if there were great crowds of adults standing in front of you, and then you'd complain."

Emily had a position at the railing, too, and noticed that a crowd was forming behind her. People were pushing a bit, and she felt a trickle of sweat drip down her back.

"You must really be hot!" Debbie said.

"You should have left your jacket on the minibus."

"No, I'm great," Emily said, wishing Debbie were back in Detroit. But she decided she didn't care what anybody thought of her clothes, she *was* leaving the jacket in the minibus next time they got out. She just wished she could figure out a way to pull off her tights!

Their little group was huddled together and watched over by the guide, who reminded Emily of a mother hen. Or maybe those collies that guard flocks of sheep. That's what Emily felt like: a sheep.

She listened to the conversations around her and decided that most of her tour group were Americans, or at least English speaking. There were a blond boy and his sister from Denmark—at least she thought they were brother and sister. They looked alike, shoved each other, and argued a lot. There was a shy

49

Chinese boy with straight black hair, who hadn't yet spoken. Two girls, Jennifer and Melanie, turned out to be American and had met each other that morning. They spent the entire time discussing why one's hometown was definitely better than the other's. There was a sandy-haired boy who spoke English with a German accent. Emily couldn't tell if he was from Germany, Austria, or Switzerland. He wasn't half bad-looking, but it was hard to understand him when he spoke. The tall boy, Roy, who seemed not to know what the Changing of the Guard was about, was American, and his seatmate, a younger boy who was very short, also seemed to be from the United States. Emily decided the tall boy wouldn't ordinarily be caught dead hanging around with that other kid.

"So let's get this show on the road already," the tall boy said rather loudly. Several grown-ups behind them laughed.

The guide looked irritated and said, "The

ceremony starts at half past eleven, with the Regimental Band and Corps of Drums playing a traditional slow march."

"Marches aren't slow," Roy corrected her.

"They can be slow, Roy," the guide said patiently. "Then there is the symbolic handing over of the keys to the palace—"

"Keys to the palace! That's just what I want!" Roy chortled, and Emily crossed her arms and turned away. "So any of those guys can get in anytime they want?"

"It's *symbolic,* Roy," the guide continued in a soft voice. "There aren't really any keys. And then . . ."

Emily tuned out. She was beginning to see what her mother meant about representing her country. Roy was an embarrassment to the U.S.A.

The two French girls were whispering to each other. They seemed to point at Emily, and then they giggled together. Emily glared at them.

In English the young French girl tried to explain. "We were just saying that the hair color you have is so—so—" She groped to find the word she meant.

"Red," Debbie offered. "Her hair is really, really red."

"Red, yes, but *chic aussi.*"

Just then the band and the drum corps began their march, and all heads turned toward the palace. Thank heaven, Emily thought.

Chapter Four

Alone for a moment, Amanda scanned the room from under her pale eyelashes. A juggler stood tossing pins in the air and catching them easily. The magician was moving about, pulling coins and toys from behind the ears of some of the children, who rewarded her with laughter. In the center of the room the table was set for tea.

Amanda undid the tiny pearl buttons on her white cardigan and slipped it off, putting it on a crimson upholstered Victorian chair that no one was ever allowed to sit on.

Amanda saw the usual party menu: sausage rolls; all sorts of little sandwiches, made

of cucumber, jam, banana, or honey; quails' eggs; éclairs; fairy cakes, cut into hearts and dusted with powdered sugar; dice cakes; lovely chocolate biscuits with multicolored rainbow hundreds and thousands; butterfly cake, with wings; and meringue nests with cream. To drink, there were the usual: black-currant juice and, of course, tea.

Amanda had seen it all many times before, but it was still beautiful. As she looked out the window at the blue sky, however, she wondered what would happen if someone announced that the doors would be opened and all the children should just run freely outside into the gardens. Wouldn't that be a brilliant idea and a stupendous birthday party! she thought.

She smiled at her cousins and their friends, though she hung back a little. Amanda thanked the magician when she pulled a flower from behind Amanda's ear and gave it to her. She managed to eat one jam sandwich and one fairy cake. She avoided most of the games, managing to beg off politely. She simply smiled and smiled and smiled.

———〰———

"Our next stop is Piccadilly and St. James's," the guide announced into her little microphone.

Emily felt lonely. The other kids on the tour were noisy, and each tried to outdo the others. Who *cared* about any of them? She had friends at home. She hadn't come to London to make new friends. She'd come to have a spring holiday with her parents, and they'd disappointed her. Work. Work. Work. She had bought a postcard from a vendor at Buckingham Palace. It showed an aerial view of the redbrick palace, with its forty-acre garden and six hundred rooms. She pulled out a pen she'd clipped to her jeans jacket and began to write to her best friend:

Dear Stacy,

This is where the Queen lives. Sometimes. My parents said I could go out on my own so I came here to visit her. Ha ha. Except I sneaked past the guard and got to watch the Royal Family having lunch. I'll tell you all about it. How was your bike trip?

Love, Emily

She tucked the postcard into her jacket pocket and clipped the pen to it. Stacy would be so bored if I told her I was on a children's tour, Emily thought. It's okay if she thinks I saw the Queen. Anyway, maybe I *will* see the Queen.

Emily dutifully got out of and into the minibus with the others and gazed blankly at the Ritz Hotel, the Burlington Arcade, and the Royal Academy. They checked out the West End, which is the theater district, and Emily hoped mightily that her parents would surprise her with tickets to see a show that night.

At last the minibus made a stop in Wellington Street for lunch. The street-level part of the two-story restaurant served American food—hamburgers and salads. Emily thought the guide must have figured everyone would like that. The American kids were happy, but the Danish brother and sister grumbled about wanting fish and chips, since they were in England.

Emily didn't care what kind of food she ate. She wasn't very hungry, although she should have been, considering how little she'd had for breakfast.

"You children please take seats over here," the guide said, waving her arm over them, "and we'll take your orders and bring you your lunches."

"The guide probably gets a kickback from the restaurant for bringing us here," Roy whispered to Debbie. "That's how it works. 'Bring us your tour, we'll pay.' My father told me all about that stuff."

Debbie gazed at Roy through her sunglasses and nodded.

Emily downgraded her opinion of Debbie. She thought Debbie and Roy deserved each other. She wondered when they'd finally get to see the Tower of London, where Anne Boleyn and Catherine Howard, two of Henry VIII's six wives, got their heads cut off. Madame Tussaud's was supposed to be pretty good, too. Stacy had told her they had life-size wax figures of famous people, like film stars and athletes and presidents and rock stars and murderers!

But it looked as if it was going to take a while to get there. The tour was going to stop at a palace or castle or something first.

Emily took out her pen and another postcard she'd bought. It showed a picture of the theater district, and that gave her an idea. She put the card on the table and began to scribble:

Dear Stacy,
    See these theaters? I'm going to a show in each one of them. A peachy English girl I met here is taking me. She's older, she's fourteen.

                       Love, Emily

Amanda had drifted over to the large French doors at one corner of the room and was staring down at the gardens below. The springtime sun was baking the flowers, and the whole garden was full of warm colors—yellow, red, pink. Of course there was green, too—lovely green grass with sunlight on it.

It looked inviting, Amanda thought. Hot,

but inviting. It isn't that far down, she thought, standing on tiptoe by the window. I could just climb right out and slide to the ground. Oh, just to be outside, on my own and free! To get rid of this silly itchy petticoat and this dress and wear shorts in the sun! She smiled to herself. Now, what would be the first thing I'd do? Well, I guess the first thing would be to lie right down in the grass and feel the sun on my face and arms, which I've *never* been allowed to do. I don't care a jot about getting more freckles anyway. And it would be smashing if I could go swimming, or wade in one of the fountains, the one where the cherub is playing with the dolphin that squirts water out of its mouth! I would pretend I was another dolphin and we were playing and—

"What *are* you doing, Amanda, Princess of Powers Court?" asked a teasing voice at her elbow.

"Why don't you behave like a proper host, Cousin George," Amanda suggested, "and let me be?"

Cousin George drew himself up to his royal posture. "I *am* a proper host." He waved his arm and indicated a young man softly strumming a guitar near the tea table. "There's your accompanist, Amanda. All my guests want to hear your lovely voice."

"Sing 'Happy Birthday' to Cousin George, Amanda," George's friend Thomas urged, winking.

"No, sing 'Rocket to the Moon,' " Cousin George said. "That new song the Mashed Potatoes do. You know, Amanda, you *love* the Mashed Potatoes!" He elbowed Thomas in the ribs.

" 'Happy Birthday' first, Amanda, as a special present for the birthday boy!" Thomas slapped Cousin George on the back.

Cousin George leaned forward, watching her. He wondered why she had such a funny look on her face. All he'd done was ask her to sing for him on his birthday. What was so awful about that? He really wanted her to sing—in fact, he expected it. Her voice was excellent. And who didn't like "Rocket to the Moon" by the Mashed Potatoes?

Amanda avoided Cousin George's gaze. She looked again for Nanny, but Nanny hadn't come back yet. She'd been gone quite a while, too. Perhaps she needed the medicine for her headaches. That had happened before. Nanny might even have fallen asleep in her rocker.

The magician had asked Jack, the chauffeur and security man, to help carry a heavy trunk. Jack was actually off his post for once.

Lucky me! Amanda smiled suddenly. There was no one at the door! There would never be a better time.

Amanda moved toward the door. Glide smoothly, she told herself, gracefully make your exit like a true princess, but hurry,

hurry, before someone pays attention and you're made to stay!

———ɯɯ———

"What's the name of this place again?" Roy asked.

"Powers Court!" Everyone said it together and laughed. The guide had mentioned the palace's name at least five times before they got there.

The other kids seemed to have paired off, but Emily didn't have a buddy. She was last and alone, but she didn't mind, not too much. These kids were just on a tour with her— she'd never be friends with them or even see them again.

Emily left her jeans jacket in the minibus with two more hastily written postcards to Stacy. One card told her friend that Emily had danced at the Hard Rock Cafe, even though Stacy knew that Emily couldn't dance and didn't even like music very much. The other card showed a picture of Derby Day at Epsom Downs, "one of the great events in the British racing calendar." Emily wrote that she had been to the races and even sat on a horse.

Without the jacket she felt cooler, and she no longer cared that the whole world would see her silly pink dress, puffed sleeves and all. The only thing she wanted to do was get through the tour and get back to the hotel. She hoped her parents were having as bad a day as she was. Then she whispered an apology for that terrible thought. Deep down she knew they loved her and probably even felt sorry that they had ruined her plans.

"This is called the Great Hall," the guide explained as their small group entered Powers Court through an arched doorway. "Notice the beautiful painted ceiling panels, which date from 1535—"

"I was just a baby then." Roy chuckled, and Debbie punched his arm. No matter where you go, Emily thought, there's a clown in every group.

"And this is the famous King's Staircase, leading to the Private Apartments. Over the centuries, kings and queens, princes and princesses, and royal cousins have lived in these rooms. Notice the fine tapestries on the walls. . . ."

Jennifer opened her eyes wide. "My mother would love those! Too fancy for my taste. I like—you know—modern stuff."

Melanie, the American girl with blond hair, agreed. "This material on the walls is so *heavy*-looking, isn't it? Do people still live here? It's too stuffy for me."

"It's extraordinary," Emily said softly to the guide. "It really is. I can just imagine kings and queens actually living in a place like this."

The guide smiled at her and then explained that the family did indeed still use these quarters. The tapestries were not only beautiful but practical. "In the old days, the drafts were such that the tapestries kept the rooms warm. Today these rooms are scheduled for state events when necessary."

Amanda couldn't believe her luck!

This corridor actually led to a way out. She knew this from the footman, Simon. She often accompanied him when he walked the dogs. Amanda looked around. No one. No one at all! This *never* happened! There was *always* someone! She shivered with a sudden feeling of joy. Freedom, real freedom!

Amanda wriggled out of the stiff, scratchy petticoat and sighed with relief as the soft pink skirt of her dress fell around her legs. She tucked the petticoat behind some drapes, on a windowsill.

Up to the ledge, hurry, hurry, and drop!

You can do it, it's not far at all, you take ballet lessons, you can do it easily, easily, *now!*

And there she was. Outside.

Where?

Amanda frowned. Just exactly where was she? In which garden and on which side? She remembered the little pond over there with the sculpture of the Greek goddess, but it had been a while since she'd been round this way. She'd been in such a hurry, she hadn't really gotten her bearings. Not that it mattered, really. All she had to do was keep walking in one direction, staying close to the walls, and she would certainly meet with something more familiar.

"Whoa, check it *out!*" Roy cried.

They were standing in a spectacular golden-red bedchamber that had a vaulted ceiling of deep yellow orange and walls cov-

ered in silk. A four-poster bed stood against the far wall, under a portrait of Queen Victoria.

"Hey, this should be *your* bedroom, Red!" Debbie called to Emily. "It's practically the color of your hair, isn't it, guys?"

They walked through three splendid rooms: the White Drawing Room, the Canaletto Room, and the Library.

"Look at that incredible dollhouse!" Jennifer said, pointing to a miniature stained-glass skylight in the magnificent gabled roof.

"Wow, I think my whole family could fit into it!" Debbie exclaimed.

"I've never seen anything as beautiful. I love dollhouses and I've seen books with gorgeous ones, but never like this one," Jennifer said. "Is this the Queen Mary dollhouse?"

"No, indeed not," the guide replied. "That dollhouse is in Windsor Castle. This one belongs to the Powers Court family.

"We're moving along, now," she continued. "It's after one o'clock already and we have so much more to see. We're about to visit the elegant dining room, designed in neoclassical style. . . ."

I won't follow them, Emily decided suddenly. As the other kids began to move out of the lovely bedroom, she lingered, eyeing the elegant bed. She noticed again the portrait of Queen Victoria. Emily felt better, less lonely, just gazing at the imposing, self-assured Queen. She tiptoed over to the dollhouse for a closer look.

Something caught her eye. Was that a *light* in one of the dollhouse rooms? Emily looked around, saw that her tour was disappearing down the corridor, and without thinking twice, stepped right over the red velvet guard rope. She crouched down on one knee and squinted hard, but she couldn't find the source of the unusual light that seemed to be coming from one of the miniature rooms.

If I stand against the wall, she said to herself, I'll be able to see it all from the top and figure this out.

She pressed herself hard against the silk-covered wall and almost lost her balance as she felt herself moving backward.

The wall was turning. Before she could stop it, she was on the other side!

With her back still against the wall, Emily found herself facing—not the golden-red bedroom, but a long gallery with dark portraits on either side.

She stood very still. Only her eyes moved from side to side.

"Uh-oh," she said.

Chapter Five

What in the world are all these people with cameras and backpacks and bags doing here? Amanda wondered as she crept along, hugging the wall, ducking behind bushes if she thought anyone even glanced her way.

She looked around again to figure out her exact whereabouts. The public area, that's right! Tourists here for the palace tour.

She moved closer to the edge of the garden. They'll just think I'm one of them, she decided. After all, there are so many people, no one will bother with one more child.

She observed people's eager faces as their groups headed to or from the palace tour. They looked so happy, Amanda almost sighed aloud. They get to wear clothes that don't itch—anything they want! she thought. Well, perhaps *that* woman really shouldn't wear pants that short. . . .

Without realizing it, Amanda had joined them. She was walking with them, listening to conversations, accents, complaints. She understood a lot of what was being said. She studied French and German with her tutors, and world history was an important part of her education. And, of course, she had had to learn the history of her family.

"Hey, there she is!" someone yelled.

Amanda whirled around. Oh, no, they've found me! she thought. They've caught me, and in front of all these strangers, too! But the faces staring at her weren't ones she knew. And they were all—children!

"Come on, Red! We've been looking everywhere for you!" This came from an odd, round girl with peculiar sunglasses.

"We're going to see the Bloody Tower!" a blond girl said with what seemed like a Scandinavian accent.

Amanda tried to remain calm and collected.

"Come along, dear," said a woman in a brown suit, who was obviously English, gesturing at her. "You had us worried." She laughed lightly. "Honestly, if it weren't for that red hair of yours, I doubt we would have spotted you so quickly in this crowd. Now, please, you'd best come! The minibus is here and our tour has a schedule. We must keep to it."

Amanda stared.

"Red! Move!" the round girl yelled, and Amanda followed the crowd of children. She couldn't believe she was going with them. But she had wanted an adventure, and she meant to have it.

Emily took a small step away from the door in the wall, drew a deep breath, and dared to glance around further.

This corridor looked a lot different from all the elegant rooms she'd seen on the tour. Somehow it looked less public, as if someone actually lived here. Emily was obviously in one of the family's hallways. She couldn't believe it. There's nothing to be afraid of, she decided, calming herself. Okay, so the wall spun around and it turned out to be a secret door. If this won't wow the kids back home, what will?

She took another step.

It's a mystery, that's what it is, she thought. I've read a million mysteries, and the girl detective is always finding secret passageways and stuff. Now *I've* found one. It's an adventure! Look at the positive side, Em, she told herself. You're in a foreign country, you're all by yourself, it's only right that you should have an adventure.

She smiled a little.

She was about to begin her exploration when she heard a laugh coming from a room off the corridor. She stopped in her tracks and held her breath.

"Hannah!" the laughing voice cried. "You're a right one, you are!" And a woman, still laughing, came out into the hall. She turned in the opposite direction from where Emily was frozen statuelike, and hurried away. She was carrying a silver tray, Emily could see, and wore a black-and-white uniform.

She's a maid, Emily thought. . . . And she didn't see me, she didn't see me at all.

Maybe she's a ghost!

Emily put her hand over her mouth to keep from crying out. She's a ghost-maid, walking around in a palace that's hundreds of years old. But who would she be serving, anyway? Everybody who lived here is dead! No, no, hold on a minute, Emily told herself. That's not true. The guide said the family still uses the palace. That maid must have been waiting on one of them!

Emily could feel her heart pounding. She continued down the corridor, taking bolder steps. I might never have another chance like this in my whole life, she thought. Here I am in an English palace, no ropes, no guides, no Mom or Dad or guards.

A curtain. Made of heavy, dark material, right next to her, right in the wall, the way the secret door had been. This would be some place to play hide-and-seek, Emily thought.

"Hurrah!" a chorus of voices cried on the other side of the curtain, and Emily jumped. She pulled the edge of the curtain aside and peeked in.

Emily had never seen such a sight! Some kind of magical party was going on. There were fabulous decorations everywhere, and a table loaded with beautiful food such as she couldn't have imagined in her wildest dreams! The kids were all dressed up—the boys were wearing jackets and ties and polished shoes. They were all staring at one corner of the room, where a magician on a tiny stage was performing tricks with real birds and bunnies.

Emily was completely caught up in the excitement. It looked like such fun. And if they *were* ghosts, they couldn't have been dead that long—those clothes looked modern!

She thought about the parties she and her girlfriends in New York City had on their birthdays. What a difference! Boys were not always invited. Sometimes a bunch of girls went skating or bowling, or maybe they had a crafts party and made jewelry or ceramics, or they went to an amusement park and went on all the rides, or they had a slumber party, where everyone slept in sleeping bags on the floor of the living room, only they didn't ever sleep, they laughed and put makeup on each other and watched scary movies and ate pizza.

Those were parties.

This was—was—

Emily couldn't find a word for what this was! The food alone was—awesome! Who were these kids, anyway?

She gently pulled the curtain aside and quietly stepped into the room.

"That's my seat," the shortest, youngest member of the tour piped up.

"That's *his* seat, Red," Roy echoed. "Can't you remember where you're supposed to be?"

Amanda smiled. "I didn't know we had to stay in the same seats," she said, rising.

"Wha—?" Debbie began, her nose wrinkling.

"Hey, 'dyou hear that?" Melanie said, nudging Jennifer.

"Listen to her," the Danish brother, Yann, said.

"That accent!" Debbie chortled, and everyone turned around in his or her seat. "Red, here, visits one English palace and she walks out with an English accent!"

Amanda blushed.

"Well, go on, Red—say something else!"

"I'm glad you like my accent," Amanda said, and curtsied in the aisle. "I think I do this rather well, don't you?"

Debbie, for once, was speechless.

"Actually, you do," Yann's sister, Liv, said. "It sounds quite authentic to me."

"Me too, let's hear some more of it," Yann said.

"Please, sit down, dear," the guide said. "The minibus can't move unless every child is sitting down with seat belt fastened."

"You may sit in my seat if you want," the youngest boy told Amanda shyly, and smiled at her.

"No, that's quite all right, thank you, it's your seat—" Amanda looked at him questioningly.

"Barry," he told her, almost whispering.

"Barry," she repeated. "That's a lovely name." She began to look around for her own seat and caught a glimpse of Debbie, holding up a jeans jacket and making a bored face at her. "I'll just go back where I belong," Amanda said, and moved down the aisle.

"So what's with you, anyway, Red?" Debbie asked. "All of a sudden you're English?"

"Well, it's—fun, isn't it?" Amanda answered brightly. "Getting in the mood of it? The tour, I mean. I was starting to be a bit bored." *What is going on here?* she wondered. *Who* are *these people? And who am* I *supposed to be?*

Debbie snorted and rolled her eyes.

"Children, we're in South Kensington," the guide announced, "and on your right there is the V and A."

"The Veterans Administration?" Roy called out.

"Veterans Administration?" Amanda repeated. She was thinking fast. Maybe if she told the story of Queen Victoria and Prince Albert, the kids wouldn't notice she wasn't who they thought she was.

"The VA. We've got one, too," Roy said. "My dad's in the army, that's why we travel so much. And I know all about the VA. This building's a whole lot bigger than any other VA I've ever seen."

"No, no," the guide said, and Debbie snickered. "This is the Victoria and Albert Museum. You've all heard of Queen Victoria?" She directed the question to Roy, who looked blank.

"I know quite a bit about Queen Victoria." Amanda spoke up without even thinking.

"She was kind. She sincerely sympathized with the joys and sorrows of her people. She was devoted to duty, she had a middle-class attitude toward social conventions, and everyone loved her for the simplicity of her character."

They all looked at Amanda. The guide seemed shocked but pleased. She covered her mouth and cleared her throat.

"I'm delighted your American school has taught you about our past," she said. "Allow me to continue. Prince Albert was the Queen's consort, her husband. He was the one who organized the Great Exhibition of 1851—that's why this building was built—and he wanted to continue his work of promoting the arts and sciences."

Amanda raised her hand and added, "Yes, Albert wasn't very popular. The Great Exhibition helped him to look and feel useful. Victoria adored him and depended upon him, but the people didn't really know how much the Queen valued him."

"Thank you," the guide said politely.

"My pleasure," Amanda answered. The others looked at her curiously, but they didn't seem to think she was being stuck-up

The minibus stopped briefly in front of the museum so that the children could look at the building's architecture as the guide described it.

"You see the central tower, shaped like a crown?" the guide asked, glancing at Amanda. "And above the main entrance there are statues of Queen Victoria and Prince Albert."

One of the French girls pointed and said, "But there are *quatre*— Oh, I must practice the English. There are *four* statues there, *non?*"

"King Edward the Seventh and Queen Alexandra," Amanda explained.

85

"Hey, you oughta go on *Jeopardy!*" Roy said. "You'd win a bundle!"

"What's *Jeopardy!*?"

"You know, the TV quiz show!" said Roy. "What's with you, Red? How come you're talking so much now, when before you were such a snob?" The minibus began to roll on. "Are you going to talk that way for the rest of the day?"

"There you are!" A good-looking boy in gray flannel slacks and a navy blazer was pointing at her. Emily turned around, but there was no one behind her. This boy was staring at *her*. "Jack!" the boy called. "She's right here!"

A man in what looked like a policeman's uniform whirled around and threw up his hands. "Princess Amanda, we've been looking everywhere for you and frantic with worry."

Emily managed to say, "F-Frantic?"

"We didn't want to alarm all the guests, but we've been searching everywhere. Why, we were just about to call Nanny!"

"Oh," Emily said. Were they really talking to *her*? Obviously, they were confusing her with someone else! Who? She shrugged. "Sorry," she answered in a very small voice.

The man brushed imaginary lint off the front of his uniform. "Yes, well. You're here now, that's what's important, isn't it?" He turned away and walked to the doorway, where he stood silently, hands behind his back.

"Where were you, Amanda?" the good-looking boy asked. "And what's happened to your dress? It looks different. Not so . . ." He made flouncing gestures with his hands.

Emily shrugged again. Amanda? This was too weird.

"We really didn't mean to tease you, you know. It was all in fun. Really!"

"Sure!" Emily shrugged again. "It's okay. Thanks."

"Pardon?"

Emily bit down on her lower lip. What should she say to this nice English boy who was gaping at her as if she'd lost her marbles?

"Amanda." He pointed to his chest with both his forefingers. "It's I—George. Cousin George? Remember? Hullo, can you hear me? You look and sound so strange!"

"Uh, no—Cousin George—I'm fine. I'm just fine. Honest."

"Amanda!" He burst out laughing. "An American accent! How did you manage that? Listen, everybody! Listen to what Amanda's learned how to do!" He beckoned with his arm, and several boys and girls came over.

"Go on—say something," Cousin George said encouragingly. "I think it's smashing, wait'll you hear."

Emily looked at the expectant, smiling faces. "What do you want me to say?"

This was greeted with laughter and applause.

"More!" Cousin George cried, clapping his hands.

"You guys are nice, you all look terrific, this is an awesome party. How's that? I've been practicing." She wondered how long she could keep this up.

"Smashing!" Cousin George repeated. "Are you still hungry? Would you like something more to eat?"

Emily was suddenly famished. She hadn't had much at breakfast *or* lunch, and the table spread out before her held the most incredibly tempting food she'd ever seen.

She moved closer to the table and tried to remember proper manners. "What do you think I should try first?"

Cousin George peered at the table. "I say—how about your favorite? Quails' eggs."

"Quails' eggs?" Emily thought she might gag.

Chapter Six

The minibus stopped at a snack bar, and eleven young tourists and a princess climbed out for a stretch and a lemonade.

There were little round tables under umbrellas. All the children brought their chairs over to Amanda's table and leaned close to her. She gracefully took what was offered—a sausage roll or something. She didn't want to turn it down. Even the guide was paying attention to her.

"So it was a real love story?" Debbie asked.

"Oh, it was. In fact, it's said that after Prince Albert died, Queen Victoria wound

his watch and laid it on the table every night until she died."

"And is that a true story?" asked the Chinese boy, whose name was Bao.

"Oh, I don't know," Amanda answered. "Perhaps one day I shall ask her." She smiled, and everyone laughed.

"She chose not to go to the opening of the Royal Albert Hall. It was too painful for her," Amanda continued. "The Prince of Wales had to do the honors, even though it opened in 1870 and Prince Albert had died nine years before." She nodded sadly.

"What did Prince Albert die of?" Melanie asked.

"Typhoid."

"Oooooh," Jennifer said. "Too bad!"

"And when did *she* die? Queen Victoria, I mean," Liv said.

"Not until 1901. She saw the turn of the century."

"Did she ever get married again?" Roy asked.

"Oh, no," Amanda said.

"My aunt got married after my uncle croaked," Roy said. "She said she wasn't going through the rest of her life without a man."

"Well, it's different for queens," Amanda said.

"I guess so," Melanie said, frowning at Roy, "and besides, Prince Albert was the love of her life. Wasn't he, Emily?"

Amanda was examining her finger; she'd scraped it while escaping from the palace.

"Emily?" Melanie repeated.

"Oh!" Amanda looked up sharply. She's talking to *me,* she thought. I thought my name was supposed to be Red. "Um, yes, quite. The love of her life, indeed yes." Okay, thought Amanda. I'm supposed to be an American girl, talking with a fake accent, telling a story about a Queen of England. If this tour doesn't end soon, I won't know *who* I am!

"Wow." Jennifer breathed a sigh. "I wish they'd teach history like that in my class back home in Fairfield. You'd make a great teacher, Emily."

"Thank you," Amanda answered, surprised.

"Yes, Emily, you really would," the guide said, patting the girl's shoulder as she stood. "And now it's time to get on the minibus again. But first I need to collect your snack money."

"Snack money?" Amanda asked. What's next? she wondered.

"Don't you remember?" Debbie said. "We buy our snacks ourselves. Everything else was prepaid by our parents."

"But—I don't have any money," Amanda said.

"Oh, come on," Debbie said. "You were

supposed to bring pocket money. You know, for snacks and souvenirs and stuff."

Amanda swallowed. "If you could let me have some of yours, I promise I'll pay you back, Debbie."

Debbie looked at her. A while ago she wouldn't have let this redheaded kid have a stick of gum! But something had happened to her. She'd become human or something.

"Sure, okay. You can pay me back when your parents pick you up," Debbie said.

"Brill." Amanda sighed. I wonder if I can fake an American accent? she thought.

—⁓—

"What made you change, Amanda?" Cousin George asked, passing something to drink.

Emily looked down at her dress. "Well—um, this one looked better, I guess," she said.

But Cousin George laughed. "No, no, not your frock. Your whole attitude! I mean, one moment you're acting as if we're all perfectly horrid, and the next you're fun to be with. What happened?"

Emily needed a minute—just a minute, *please,* to collect her thoughts. This really cute guy with the English accent was actually talking to her as if he *knew* her. He called her—what?—Amanda? How could he possibly know her? She would certainly have remembered if she'd ever seen *him* before.

No, of course she hadn't seen him before. Or any of the others. And yet they knew her.

No, wait. They knew *Amanda,* not Emily Jane Chornak from Brooklyn Heights. *Who was she supposed to be, anyway?*

"Amanda?" Cousin George was looking at her oddly.

Emily wiped her brow with the back of her hand. "Gee, I'm sorry—uh—Cousin George. I guess—I mean, the heat or something—"

"Oh, just a moment, I will get you a

chair." He grabbed the nearest one and pulled it over for her.

Emily sank into it. She had used faintness as an excuse, but she *was* feeling a little dizzy. Amanda *who*?

"Cousin George?"

"Yes! Are you all right?"

"Listen, Cousin George, just for the fun of it—"

"What?" Cousin George was always ready for fun.

"Let's play a game, okay?" Emily suggested.

"Oh, yes! What kind?"

I hope this doesn't sound too stupid, she thought, and plunged ahead anyway. "You are my cousin—"

"Yes."

"Cousin George."

"Right. . . ."

"Uh-huh, and now you say your last name."

Cousin George tilted his head. "You mean my full title?"

"Right! Your full title!"

"Well, all right. . . . I'm George Christian Henry Edward Milford, Lord Smythe."

Emily swallowed. Whoa, he's a lord, she thought. Well, sure, he would be, I mean, he lives in a palace, he must be. So what am I, then? If I'm a cousin, then I must be somebody, too!

Cousin George was tapping his foot. "What's the game, Amanda? I've said who I am, what happens now?"

"Now you say who *I* am," Emily said, looking at him encouragingly.

"Come on now!"

"No, really. Make believe I'm a stranger, a visitor from America. A tourist. I don't know anything about this place. So who am I? You explain."

Cousin George wrinkled his nose. "This is

a strange game, Amanda. I don't see its point, really."

"*Please,* Cousin George, say who I am!" Emily begged.

"Oh, very well." He recited: "You are Princess Amanda of Powers Court."

Yow! Princess Amanda of Powers Court! That's *here.* That's *this* place. Powers Court! And I'm the Princess in the palace. Mom told me to take notes on this tour, but what am I supposed to write about *this?*

"Amanda? You really are acting quite strangely."

Well, you would be, too, Emily thought, if you'd just heard what I just heard. I think this has to be a dream, she decided. She pinched herself. "Ow!" she said.

"Amanda, should I call Nanny?" Cousin George asked.

"Hey, no. No, I'm fine, honest. Look, Cousin George—"

"Are you really fine?" he asked.

"Sure. No kidding, really."

"Good," he said, "because I'm going to open my presents now and I especially want to see what *you've* brought me."

"Me too," Emily whispered. I cannot *believe* this, she thought. I'm supposed to be an English princess, acting like an American kid. Get me outta here!

Debbie sank heavily onto the minibus seat. "I'm wiped!" she sighed.

"Wiped?" Amanda asked. She was bright-eyed and alert.

"You know—tired. Cooked. Finished."

"Wiped."

"Yeah. Aren't you?"

Amanda wasn't. She was having a wonderful time. "How did you like the Tower?" she asked. They had just visited the gray-brown, centuries-old stone symbol of London's past.

It had always been one of Amanda's favorite places.

"It was so cool," Debbie said. She leaned against the backrest and closed her eyes. "But I didn't know the Tower of London was a bunch of towers, not just one."

"Oh, yes. The White Tower, the Bloody Tower, Beauchamp Tower—"

"I liked the Bloody Tower. That mean old King killed those two little boys there, just so he could be King instead of them?"

"That's what Shakespeare wrote," Amanda said. *"Richard III."*

"Shakespeare. He wrote *Romeo and Juliet,* right?"

"Yes. Another tragic story," Amanda answered.

"Well, I saw that play," Debbie told her proudly. "My mother took me to see it in Chicago in February."

"Really! Did you like it?"

"Aw, I didn't really understand it. They

liked each other but their parents didn't or something and then he died and then she died because he died."

Amanda laughed. "Well, I guess you got the gist of it, anyway," she said.

"You're nicer since you started doing that accent," Debbie said, and yawned.

Amanda wiggled around in her seat. She had been sitting on Emily's jacket, and it had begun to bother her. She pulled it out from under her and felt a bulge in the pocket. She unzipped the pocket and pulled out a denim wallet. The wallet was folded in three and held together by a strip of Velcro.

Amanda looked at Debbie, who seemed to be sleeping. She looked again at the wallet.

I don't mean to snoop, she thought. This is awful of me, but—I should find out just who I am—or rather, who they *think* I am.

She pulled the Velcro apart.

Inside were several little plastic windows with photographs in them—a redheaded girl

102

standing in front of a tall man and a shorter woman, with a pretty row house behind them. Amanda could hardly see the girl's face because she was wearing sunglasses, and besides, the picture was mostly of the house. But the girl did have startling red hair. Just like mine, Amanda thought.

There was a photo of a smiling older woman with glasses and brown hair. Grandmama, perhaps?

Oh! A picture of a dog—a puppy! How wonderful! The puppy was on a bed with a pink bedspread. He seemed to be curled up with a teddy bear right next to the pillow. Amanda had dogs, too, Pekingese, but they never slept on her bed. Actually, they were never allowed in her room. Simon, the footman, looked after them.

Amanda turned to the last item in the plastic windows. An identification card!

Emily Jane Chornak, Brooklyn Heights, New York.

New York!

The Statue of Liberty, the Empire State Building, Times Square, the United Nations, *Broadway!* Amanda's head swam. Her parents had been to New York City, but she never had. They'd brought back souvenirs. Amanda's favorite was a glass paperweight with a tiny Statue of Liberty inside; when you turned it upside down, it snowed, and it played music. She'd looked at the beautiful picture book of New York City with full-page color photographs. She knew that Manhattan was an island because one of the most wonderful pictures was taken from the air and you could see the rivers on each side—now what were their names?

She almost woke Debbie up to ask her, but Debbie wasn't from New York City and she might not know.

Anyway, she was Emily Jane Chornak, and she came from New York City! Was

Brooklyn Heights in New York City? Of course, it had to be. Imagine living in New York City as an ordinary person and seeing all those wonderful sights anytime you wanted to!

As Amanda put the wallet back into the jacket pocket, she felt another object on the other side. She lifted the material and saw several postcards jammed into another pocket. It's very wrong to read someone else's post, she thought, and patted the jacket down with both hands.

Where had the guide said the minibus was stopping? Wasn't it Victoria Station? She peered out of the window. They were almost there.

Oh, bother, it's supposed to be *my* jacket, anyway, she said to herself, and took out the postcards. I need to do this, she told herself, because I need to know as much as possible about who I am!

She began to read.

Oh, my! This girl Emily saw the Queen at lunch by sneaking past the guard! She sounds quite like me! Amanda giggled. I say! She's seen every show in Soho and Covent Garden? Now, how could she have ridden a horse at Epsom Downs?

Amanda frowned. Perhaps she's made it all up so that her friend at home will be impressed with her visit here. Oh, I certainly would love to meet this Emily Jane Chornak someday. We would have a lot to talk about, wouldn't we? I wonder where *she* is now? Suddenly Amanda had a thought. Was it possible . . . no, of course not. There was no way Emily Chornak could be at Powers Court. Could she?

Amanda came out of her reverie as she noticed that the minibus had stopped. The children were gathering their things together. Amanda could see excited parents trying to peer into the minibus windows to catch a glimpse of their children. Some of them were waving and calling.

Now Amanda was beginning to be frightened. These children might not have known Emily Jane Chornak well enough to recognize her easily, but Emily's own parents certainly would!

Emily felt like Cinderella.

No, she *was* Cinderella. Everyone thought she was a princess at the ball, and she really was a fifth-grade kid from New York who didn't have even one servant, unless you counted Irma from the neighborhood, who came in to do the heavy cleaning once a week. And if she ever called Irma a servant, she'd probably get a smacked bottom!

"Come now, Amanda, it's time!"

Emily turned. Cousin George was standing there looking at her expectantly.

"Time for what?" she asked.

"*You* know! Thank you for the puzzle, it's a proper gift, but when do I get the grand present I asked you for earlier?"

Emily wrinkled her nose. *What* present? What was he talking about?

"Oh, Amanda, the *song,* of course! First 'Happy Birthday' and then our favorite— 'Rocket to the Moon'!"

"Rocket to the Moon!" Emily had certainly heard of that! Her parents had played it constantly at home before they'd all left for Europe. It was sung by that stupid group with some dumb vegetable name. She'd heard it often enough, she should remember it—the Fried Tomatoes? No, but it was some food. . . .

"Amanda?"

"Yes?"

"I've been waiting all afternoon. You must sing for us, please!"

Sing for them? Oh, good grief!

"I—uh—I can't, Cousin George. I mean,

I'd love to, really, but I really can't. My throat." She coughed twice. "See? Bad throat. Bad!" She coughed again. How could she sing? The music teacher at home wouldn't even let her join the school chorus! She couldn't carry a tune, and besides, there was quite enough music in her family, thank you very much!

"Amanda, it's my birthday." Cousin George was almost pleading. "It would mean so much to me. Please."

Emily licked her lips. Think, Emily, think. How could she distract him? What could she do that he'd like instead of (ugh!) singing?

"Cousin George!"

"What?"

"I can hold my breath for over a minute!" She could, too. She'd done it at camp, learning to swim. "Look, Cousin George, none of the other kids could do it!" She inhaled deeply and noisily. Cousin George's mouth opened in astonishment.

Some of the other guests came over as Emily's face turned bright red and her cheeks puffed out.

"I say, Cousin George, what's Amanda doing?" a girl whispered.

"Holding her breath," he answered.

"Why?"

Cousin George shrugged.

The room grew silent, and Emily's face got redder.

"Amanda, I think you're going to faint," Cousin George said, frowning.

But Emily shook her head wildly as her eyes widened in concentration.

"She looks sort of odd, doesn't she," Thomas whispered to Cousin George.

Cousin George nodded.

"Do you think she's going to do this for much longer?" Thomas asked.

Cousin George shrugged.

"Phooo-oooo-oooooo!" Emily finally exhaled loudly and stood gasping for breath.

"How—How long was it?" she managed between breaths.

"How long was what?" Thomas asked.

"How long did I hold it? My breath? The last time I tried it, it was one minute, two seconds. But I was lying on my bed at the time, so maybe it was easier, you know, because I was more relaxed. So how long was it?"

"I haven't any idea," Cousin George said, shrugging again.

"You didn't time it? Oh, no! You mean I have to do it *again*?"

"Why, no—"

"This is a joke, isn't it, Amanda!" a girl named Alexis interrupted, clapping her hands. "How funny! What an idea, really, holding your breath!"

"A joke, of course!" Cousin George cried, smiling. "Smashing, Amanda, really. Now, sing!"

"Wait!" Emily racked her brain. "Do you

know what else I can do? I can—I can . . . Oh! Listen! I'm double-jointed!"

"I say, are you all right? This American bit is funny, but you seem a bit daft. Are you feeling quite well?"

"Yes! I am! Watch." She plopped onto the floor with her knees bent in front of her in a frog-legged position. Then she leaned back . . . back . . . back, until she was lying flat, with the bottoms of her feet touching each side of her waist.

The party guests stood over her, staring.

No one spoke. "Double-jointed," Emily repeated lamely. "Of course, I usually do the real good stuff wearing tights. . . ."

Everyone stared at her.

Whoa, she thought. It's not easy being Cinderella. And I wonder where the real Princess is, anyway?

A fancy clock on the mantel caught her eye. Speaking of Cinderella! It was after three, which meant that the tour would be

over and people would be looking for her! She'd have to duck out of here the way Cinderella did at the stroke of midnight. But Emily had to smile a bit, thinking that she should have worn glass slippers so that she could leave one near the door for Cousin George to find!

"Amanda, I'm going to ask the musician if he can play 'Rocket to the Moon,' all right? Amanda?"

Emily sighed. She hated to be rude, but she had to leave!

"Cousin George," she began, "this was a lovely party—"

"You aren't leaving!"

"I must, I really must. My throat." She coughed again, weakly. "I wouldn't want you or the other guests to catch anything. You know, in case I'm coming down with something."

"I quite understand, if you aren't feeling well. . . ."

"Thanks for inviting me," she said, wondering if she was supposed to shake his hand or bow or something.

Cousin George laughed. "You're quite welcome!"

No, she was a princess, she didn't have to bow! Now, which way was out? She hadn't come through a door before, had she? She'd come from that funny hallway through a curtain.

There! It was over there, at the back of the room! If she could just make her way over there without attracting any more attention . . .

She smiled at Cousin George and began to move away.

"Amanda?" he called after her.

She winced, turned, waved, then walked away as quickly as she could without running.

Chapter Seven

At last, Victoria Station. Amanda knew the station. She could easily get a taxi here and pay for it at Powers Court. But what about the two waiting parents? Even assuming she could sneak out of the minibus without being spotted—drat this hair!—all these children and the guide would say she had been right with them and where could she have gotten to? The poor guide would be blamed. Oh, dear.

She looked wildly about, but there didn't seem to be any help for it. She chewed her lip. What to do?

"One moment, children, one moment!" The guide was making an announcement. The group in the minibus grew silent, and each child turned toward the front. "Emily? Where are you, dear? Oh, there!"

Amanda stared, wide-eyed.

"Emily, your parents rang our office to say that they wouldn't be able to fetch you. It was business, they said, and you'd understand because you knew all about it."

Amanda almost cried with relief. Part of her felt sad for Emily, the only child whose parents hadn't come. But Amanda knew all about promises from busy parents, and she guessed that Emily Jane Chornak probably did, too. And there was another part of her that could scarcely contain her glee! No one was here! She was free.

"But," the guide said, gesturing over the heads of the children, "they did say they were sending a car to collect you and bring you back to your hotel. Emily? Did you get that, dear?"

A car! Fan-*tas*-tic!

"Yes, I did! Thank you so much!"

"But wait, dear, there's more. Come here and I'll tell you the rest of the message."

Amanda looked up at the guide. More?

"Yes, they said that once you get to the hotel they want you to have a wash and change your clothes to something more comfortable. Then tell the concierge to put you in a taxi for Number One-oh-one Ardsmore Lane. Don't you want to write this down, dear?"

"Um . . ." Amanda fumbled with the denim jacket and pulled out Emily's pen and one of the postcards. She only pretended to write. Anyone could remember Number One-oh-one Ardsmore. And besides, she wouldn't be going there, anyway. She had to get back to Powers Court.

118

Ardsmore . . . What was it she'd heard about Ardsmore? Oh, yes! Amanda smiled. There was a nightclub in Ardsmore Lane. She'd read it on the Mashed Potatoes album, in the liner notes. The club . . . Archie's? Yes, it was Archie's. A small nightclub in Ardsmore Lane, she'd read, where the Mashed Potatoes first worked together. Well, she'd had enough of being Emily, the American tourist. Time to go . . .

She stood up quickly, and Emily's wallet slipped from the pocket and fell to the floor. Debbie picked it up, and as she handed it over, Amanda suddenly thought, Maybe . . .

She opened the wallet again and looked into its back folds. An American five-dollar bill and a twenty-pound note.

"I say, Debbie, here you are!" she cried, handing Debbie the American bill. "For the snack. I owe it to you!"

"Well, yeah, but it wasn't this much—"

"No, that's quite all right. I don't have anything smaller, so don't worry about it. I was going to ask for your address so that I could have it posted to you because my parents aren't here, but now we won't have to do that, will we?"

"Uh . . . ," Debbie said, stuffing the bill into her pocket. "Y'know, Red—I was going to ask for your address anyway. You're okay, you know? I thought we could write to each other."

Roy leaned over the back of his seat. "Me too. I don't do much writing, but listen—if I'm ever in New York sometime, why don't I give you a call?"

Amanda looked around in astonishment. She smiled at them all. "Well," she said, "I can't give you my address, actually, because"—she took a breath—"because we're moving shortly, you see, and I don't quite have the new one yet. But I'll tell you what, if you each write your own name and address down for me, I shall find *you* when we're, uh—settled. And I'll write and tell you where we are."

Debbie nudged her with her elbow. "Hey, Red?"

"Yes?"

"You oughta keep that accent. It really works for you."

Each child scribbled down his or her address while the anxious parents crowded together near the door of the minibus.

And amid cries of "How was it?" in four different languages, Amanda slipped away from the group.

She saw the car—a big black one, parked at the curb. Leaning against its side was a uniformed man holding a sign that read EMILY C.

"Well, there's my carriage," Amanda said to herself with a grin. She waved at the man, and he opened the door for her.

They had gone only a short way when

Amanda straightened her shoulders and leaned forward.

"I should like to go to Powers Court, please," she said in her most grown-up voice.

"Pardon?"

Amanda spoke more loudly.

"Powers Court, please!"

"Powers Court? No, no, miss, I'm to take you to the Beresford Hotel."

"Yes, yes, I understand, but there's been a change in plans. We're going to Powers Court."

"No one told me of a change, miss."

Amanda moved so that her reflection was visible in the driver's mirror.

"Do you know who I am?" she asked.

He looked up.

"Well, ah—"

"Never mind," she said, and opened Emily's wallet. "Please," she said politely as she handed the twenty-pound note over the seat, "I need to go to Powers Court."

The car made a U-turn, and Amanda sat back and relaxed.

"Here we are, miss. Powers Court." He opened his door to get out, but Amanda stopped him.

"This is the main gate," she said.

"Yes, miss."

"No, no, no. Take me round to the service entrance, please."

He looked at her oddly, but he nodded, shut his door again, and drove around the corner.

When he stopped, Amanda thanked him. "No, please, don't bother to get out, I'll open my own door." She did it before he could even move.

Without looking back, she walked quickly down the path to her left that led to the family quarters. It must be half past three, she thought, or quarter to four. Simon will be walking the Pekes about now.

She felt a giddy little thrill. There he was!

"Simon? Simon!" she called, beginning to run. "Over here!"

"Oh, Princess Amanda! What are you doing there?" He began to walk toward her.

The dogs barked happily, and Amanda slid to the ground and hugged all three together, laughing as they licked her face.

"Are you all right?" Simon asked worriedly.

"Quite, Simon, thank you. Can you, shall we say, sneak me in through a side door, please?"

He smiled down at her. "Of course, but may I know what you might have been up to?"

She grinned back at him. "I don't think so, Simon," she replied.

"Very well, I'll do as you request." And he winked.

Emily had gone a few yards down the corridor when she stopped.

"This wasn't it," she said out loud. "I don't remember those beams jutting out like that."

She turned and walked in the other direction. This isn't good, she thought. I don't have a clue what time it is, but if the tour is over and the minibus is wherever it's supposed to be, then what will my parents be thinking? And doesn't everyone stop to have tea or something at four o'clock? And how am I going to get out of here, anyway?

She stopped walking.

Okay, she told herself, don't panic. You got in here, you can get out. It was that room with the dollhouse that had the secret door in it. If you push it or press against it, it turns around. So all you have to do is find something that looks like it might be a secret door and just push it.

No. Wait a minute. She whirled around.
There's another corridor that goes that way
. . . and one that goes *that* way . . . and
another that . . . Ohmygosh, it's like spokes
on a wheel! How am I ever going to find my
way out? I could be trapped here forever! I
could starve to death here! I could wander
around these halls for the rest of my life,
growing older and older. . . . I could use a
bag of bread crumbs, she thought ruefully.
She almost started to cry. Then she heard a
familiar noise.

Dogs barking!

Dogs go outside, don't they? Even dogs
that live in palaces go outside, right? Find the
dogs and you'll find the outside. Emily Jane,
move!

The sound of the dogs grew louder. Emily
could tell they weren't very big. Their voices
were yippy and shrill. Suddenly they were
very close.

Emily ducked into an alcove as a uniformed man walked briskly by with three leashes attached to three small dogs. He went by without seeing her, and as soon as he was far enough away, she headed for where she thought he had come from.

Oh, boy, she thought. Here come more footsteps. I don't know who this is, but it looks like these corridors are busy enough that I probably won't be lost forever in them. Ah, here's another alcove to hide in until *this* person passes. . . .

Emily ducked into the alcove, held her breath, and pressed her back as tightly as she could against the wall. She closed her eyes, hoping that if she couldn't see anyone, then no one could see her.

The footsteps stopped in the middle of the hall.

Uh-oh, Emily thought.

No one moved. Emily didn't dare breathe. Come on, she thought, whoever you are, just keep on going to wherever you have to go.

Silence.

Then, a small voice: "Come out now, whoever you are!"

Small, but commanding, Emily thought.

"This is Princess Amanda! I order you to come out now! I know there's someone hiding here!"

Princess Amanda. Emily squeezed her two hands together, threw back her shoulders, and . . .

. . . stepped out into the corridor.

Face-to-face stood two girls in pink dresses—though each dress was a little crumpled now. Both girls wore black patent leather shoes and white tights; both had hair as coppery bright as sunlight. They stood staring at each other where the spokes of the wheel of corridors met in the center.

For a few seconds, neither spoke.

Then they began to chatter.

"You're Princess Amanda—"

"Can you possibly be Emily Jane Chornak—"

"I can't believe you're really—"

"I can't believe how much we look like each other—"

"Look at our clothes—"

"Look at our *clothes*!"

"Wait a minute, wait a minute!" Emily let out a long breath and held up her hand. "This is too much," she finally managed.

"Quite!" Amanda agreed.

"Listen, I'm sorry. I hope you're not really angry. It wasn't that I *wanted* to pretend to be you, it's just that everyone *thought* I was you, so I had to *act* like I was you! I mean—gee, this is so weird, I don't even *know* what I mean. Hey, wait a minute. You called me Emily Jane Chornak!"

Amanda nodded.

"How did you know my name?" Emily asked.

Amanda laughed. "We both pretended to

130

be each other, I guess! Look, here's your jacket." She had had it draped over one shoulder, and now she pushed it at Emily. "I'm afraid I've spent all your money, but your wallet's in it, and that had—"

"All my ID!" Emily exclaimed. "This whole day has been a *movie*!"

Amanda smiled. "A bit like your post-cards?" she asked softly.

Emily blushed.

"Oh, no." Amanda touched her lightly on the arm. "Please don't be upset or angry. I didn't mean to read them, really, but I did need to know as much about you as I could! I never read anyone else's post, truly I don't! But I would have felt terribly guilty if I hadn't told you," she added.

"Oh, it's okay," Emily said, and smiled. "I did make that stuff up because what I was doing was so boring! Stacy was going on an organized bike trip on her own, without her mom and dad."

"But Emily, *you* were going to Europe!"

"I know, I know, but I was with my parents, they're agents in the music business and they're always busy so I hardly ever see them, and all I'd be doing besides this dumb kiddie tour would be sitting around our hotel room watching TV and playing solitaire!"

Amanda nodded through Emily's explanation. "Well, look what you have done, though. You've actually *been* a princess! Stacy won't think you're boring now!"

Emily nodded, too, and they both laughed. "But what happened at the end of the tour?" Emily asked, suddenly frightened. "Did my parents—?"

"No," Amanda said, shaking her head sympathetically. "They were delayed. They couldn't come. They sent a car for you, which I took here."

"Right," Emily sighed. "It figures."

"I know how you feel."

"You do?"

"I do. But wait a minute—Emily Jane?" Amanda said, suddenly curious.

"What?"

"Did you say your parents were in the *music* business?"

Chapter Eight

Crash!

"What was that?"

Startled, both girls swiveled around, eyes wide.

Amanda released a breath. "It's all right. Someone just dropped a tray in one of the kitchens, that's all. But I think we should leave these corridors." She grabbed Emily by the hand.

"Where are we going?" Emily asked, skipping to keep up.

"Just follow me," Amanda said as she hurried along. "You have to know where you're going when you come into these back corridors or you can really get lost."

"I know. . . ."

"Well, that's because they were built that way. There are tons of secret passageways no one can even see unless you push a certain button or move something like a picture or a chest."

No kidding, Emily thought.

"Yes, it was so that people could escape from their enemies easily in olden times. You know, if they were being attacked or something like that."

Or even in *these* times, Emily thought. Aloud, she said, "Isn't it late? I was supposed to be with this tour group and my parents will be waiting for me. Did you say *one* of the kitchens?"

"Shhh!" Amanda said, putting her finger to her lips. They had reached a door that led to the family quarters.

"This is where I live," Amanda said, opening it. "Let's go to my rooms and talk. There are lots of things I'd love to know! Come on, Emily!"

"Well, there are plenty of things I want to know, too," Emily said, "but I think I'll be in a bunch of trouble if I don't get back to my hotel pretty soon." Still, she was looking around as they walked. These rooms! she thought. Wow!

"Listen, Emily," Amanda said, tugging her hand. "Your parents sent more in that message to the tour company. They said they wanted you to change clothes at the hotel and take a taxi to Ardsmore Lane."

"Oh. Well . . . okay. I wonder what's going on in Ardsmore Lane?"

"Let's find out!" Amanda was practically jumping up and down.

"Why? What's so exciting?"

"Let's check on Nanny first," Amanda said. She opened a door softly and then closed it again. "Nanny's sleeping," she told Emily. "I thought she might be. Come with me."

"Your room is beautiful, Amanda. I mean Princess. What am I supposed to call you, anyway?"

"Amanda will be fine. And I'm glad you like my room. I hardly ever have anyone in here, except for Nanny."

"Oh. No sleepovers?"

"Sleepovers?"

"You know. Other kids sleeping over on the floor. In sleeping bags."

Amanda looked blank.

"Makeup? Horror movies? Pizza? No, I guess not. Is it lonely being a princess?"

Amanda nodded. "Sometimes. I'd love to spend some time with my parents, but they're—"

"—always busy!" Emily finished for her.

"Always busy. I told you I know how you

feel. But listen, Emily. We were talking about Ardsmore Lane!"

"We were?"

"Yes, yes. Let me ring them at this address and see what they say is going on there to-night."

Emily didn't much care what was going on there that night, but she watched Amanda as she picked up her telephone. Emily decided that she'd rather spend her evening right here! Amanda was easily as much fun as Stacy or any of Emily's other friends. Maybe more fun. And besides, Amanda was a real princess and this was a real palace. Emily couldn't have made up a postcard like this!

"I knew it!" Amanda suddenly cried. "Emily, come here, come here!" She was gesturing wildly with her arm.

Emily climbed down from Amanda's beautiful bed, where they had been sitting. "What's going on?"

"It's *Archie's*! I just knew it would be!

When you said your parents were in the music business, I had a feeling—" She held up her hand. "Wait a minute," she said, and turned back to the phone. "Yes. I'm calling for the Princess of Powers Court. The gentleman I just spoke to said he couldn't tell me what was happening at your club tonight, that it was private. A private concert." She paused and rolled her eyes. "No, I am not joking. What do you mean prove it to you? You must just believe me." She looked at Emily and shook her head in frustration. "He hung up!" Amanda said in utter disbelief.

"Look, let me try," Emily said. "Get the number again." Amanda punched in the number, and in a moment Emily said into the phone, "Emily Chornak here. My parents are supposed to be at your club." She waited and listened. "Chor-nak," she repeated. "Helen and Daniel. Dan. Helen and Dan Chornak." She covered the mouthpiece and turned to Amanda. "He's checking." They waited. "Hello? Yes. No, I don't need to speak to them, but can't you just tell me what's happening there tonight?" To Amanda: "He says it's a big surprise. I'll be thrilled." Back to the phone: "I don't like surprises. I mean, I do, but not this one. Please tell me and I'll never tell them you told." She looked at Amanda's face. Then she nodded as she listened. "Uh-huh, uh-huh, I kind of thought so. Thanks so much." She hung up.

"Well?" Amanda asked excitedly. "Is it really who I think it is?"

"Who do you think it is?"

"The Mashed Potatoes, silly! Is it?"

Emily's eyes widened. "How'd you know?"

"How did I *know*? I *love* them, doesn't everybody? They are the group we hear on the radio constantly. Don't you love them?"

"Not really," Emily told her. "I'm not into music."

Now it was Amanda's turn to be shocked.

Her jaw dropped. "You mean your parents are talking right now with *the Mashed Potatoes* and you don't *care*?"

Emily sat down again.

"I told you," she said to Amanda. "My parents *live* with music and music people day and night. They're always breaking appointments with me. Like today. We couldn't take a tour together because they're trying to get the Mashed Potatoes to sign with them. To be their American agents."

"Oh, I can't believe it!" Amanda cried. "That is so exciting!"

"No, it's not. It's what I live with. Now, this—*this* is exciting!" She waved her arm around the room.

"No, it's not," Amanda said. "It's what I live with."

"Our parents have responsibilities," Amanda was explaining. "We have to understand."

"*Tell* me about it."

"Why don't I tell you about what it was like being you on the minibus?" Amanda giggled. "It was lovely! We went to the Tower of London—"

"Nuts! I really wanted to see that!" Emily burst out.

"Oh, you will, I'll see to it. And we saw the Victoria and Albert Museum—well, the outside, anyway. They seemed surprised I knew so much about Queen Victoria."

"No, Amanda, they were surprised that *I* knew so much about her."

"Oh, I suppose that's true, isn't it?" Amanda laughed. "And all the time you were here at Powers Court—"

"At Cousin George's party—"

"You *didn't*! That horrid party? And those boring boys?"

"It wasn't! They weren't! I had a great time!"

Amanda sank onto her bed, her hand over

her mouth. "I don't believe it! You *enjoyed* it?"

"It was terrific! I never went to a party like that before. But what about you? You got stuck with all those boring kids for that whole time!"

"They were sweet!" Amanda nodded toward Emily's jeans jacket. "And I got all their names and addresses for you, so you can keep in touch! They're in your pocket."

"No way!"

"Oh, but you must, Emily. I promised I'd write and let them know my 'new' address in New York. They think you're quite grand. You must write to them."

"Well, your cousin and his friends think you're pretty cool, too, Amanda. We got along great!"

Amanda shook her head. "Cousin George teases me horribly. He hates me."

"But he likes your American accent now!"

There was a quick knock on the door.

Emily and Amanda looked at each other.

"Who is it?" Emily whispered.

"It could only be Nanny," Amanda whispered back, "but she'd just knock and come in. . . ."

"Amanda?" a voice called from the hallway.

"Oh! Oh, Emily! It's Cousin George!" Amanda whispered hoarsely.

"Oh, no! What'll we do?"

A mischievous look came into Amanda's eye. "I'm going behind that desk over there. You tell him to come in."

"No, Amanda, I couldn't!"

"Of course you can! You did it before."

"That was different."

"Emily, you can't know how awful he is to me, really! This is my one chance to do something back to him. *Please,* Emily, *please!*"

"But—what will I say?"

"It doesn't matter! Say anything! I'll jump out at the proper time. And then we'll watch his face!"

"*Amanda?*" Cousin George called, and rapped again on the door.

Amanda gave Emily a little push and hurried away to hide.

"Uh . . . C-Cousin G-George?" Emily stammered.

"May I come in, Amanda?"

"Well . . . sure."

The door opened, and Amanda's cousin stepped hesitantly into the room.

"I say, are you feeling better?" he asked.

"Oh, yeah—*yes,* I mean. I really had a great time at your party, I did. I mean—thanks."

"You're quite welcome. I just came to say—well, I wanted to say—I *do* like that American accent, you know!"

Emily blushed.

"But what I wanted to say was—with the

accent, you know, you—you've changed a bit, too. Don't you know."

Emily looked toward Amanda's hiding place.

"Maybe . . . ," she managed.

"No, you're *quite* changed, really! After that frog thing this morning, I thought you'd be perfectly horrid all day, but actually—well—you're not!"

"Thank you."

"You see, I've always thought you were a good cousin, even though we've played some tricks on each other—"

"Blagghhh!" The loud sound seemed to fill the room.

"What was *that*?" George asked.

But Emily jumped in quickly. "George," she said, standing to face him, "I guess I didn't know that you really liked me. But I suppose . . . if you give someone *half* a chance, you might find out that she's *twice* as nice as you thought!"

That was the moment Amanda chose to reveal herself.

Cousin George nearly jumped out of his skin. His eyes became twice their normal size. He looked from one girl in pink to the other and kept gulping air as if he couldn't quite take it in.

"This is my friend from America, George," Amanda said in an amused voice. "Her name is Emily. I suppose we look somewhat alike, so that you mistook her for me. So sorry!" She practically sang it.

George stood, sputtering.

Emily took a deep breath. "Listen, George," she blurted out, "I really did have a good time at your party. And I really think you're nice. So . . . anyway . . . thanks again. Okay?"

Amanda was grinning from ear to ear. "Good trick, wasn't it, Cousin?" she asked playfully.

George tried to regain his composure. He

nodded, smiling sheepishly at both girls. "The best," he admitted, and shaking his head, he moved slowly toward the door. He turned back and pointed a finger at Amanda. "But I'll get you!" he said, still smiling. "Oh, I'll get you back, Amanda, I will! And you *are* nice, Emily," he added as he left.

"That's for the frog!" Amanda called after him, and burst out laughing. "It was a good trick," she said to Emily, "wasn't it?"

"I think he appreciated it," Emily answered. "Artistically speaking."

As they smiled at each other, there was another knock at the door, and as Amanda had said she would, Nanny walked right in. She looked calm and refreshed until she saw Emily. Then her jaw dropped.

"Why, Amanda, who—who is this young lady?" she stammered.

"She's my friend from the United States, Nanny. Her name is Emily Jane Chornak."

"Why—she could almost be your twin!

But what's going on? What is she doing here?"

"Oh, do you think we look alike?" Amanda asked innocently, and Emily nearly choked. "Emily's parents are over here on business, and she dropped by. You were asleep and I didn't disturb you. Nanny, may we have our tea here, please?"

Nanny glared at Emily disapprovingly, then turned to Amanda. "I didn't know anything about a visit, nor did Jack—and quite frankly, well, I mean this is all quite unsatisfactory. Will this young person's parents be coming to collect her? Do they know where to come? I just don't know what your father's going to say when he returns from Scotland. I've never in all my years had such a situation." Nanny turned on her heel. "I'll be back in a moment or two," she said, and walked away.

"Is she going to call your parents?" Emily

asked. "Are you in trouble? I'd better get going. I really shouldn't stay for tea," she added sadly. "I have to go change and meet my parents at that silly club."

"Please stay a little longer," Amanda said. "I'll tell you what—I'll lend you something to wear and you can meet your parents without having to go to the hotel to change."

"I couldn't borrow your clothes, could I?"

"Yes, Emily! I like you so much, I feel as if we're old friends. The only thing I can't believe is that you don't like music!"

Emily shrugged. "I never got into it," she said.

"I adore it! All kinds!"

"I'm bored by it. All kinds."

Amanda sat back in her chair. "I believe you're prejudiced because you think of music as a bad thing. You're jealous."

"Maybe so, but that's how it is," answered Emily.

"Well, Emily, you need to start thinking about music all on its own. I know you'll learn to love it!"

Emily sighed. "I wish *you* were going to this concert tonight instead of me. My parents always put strangers—like the Mashed Potatoes—ahead of me."

"They've given you a grand opportunity, Emily. *I wish I could go!*" Amanda cried. "But even though no one seemed to be able to tell us apart, your parents certainly would."

"Mmm," Emily said thoughtfully. Then she jumped up. "Amanda!"

"Yes?"

"Let's *both* go!"

"What?"

"I said, let's both go to the concert! Together!"

"How? They'd never let me go to a rock concert! I may have escaped for a few hours, but I don't see how I could manage it again!"

The door opened, and Nanny arrived with the tea, pushing it in on a silver cart.

"Miss Nanny?" Emily ventured.

Amanda giggled, and Nanny's eyebrows arched.

"Yes, Miss Emily?"

"We were wondering—Amanda and I— if she might accompany me this evening. We're to meet my parents and listen to a concert."

"A concert? A musical?" Nanny asked, eyebrows still raised.

"Yes!" Amanda cried. "A musical! Oh, Nanny, you know how I adore music! Emily's parents are—"

"They're artists' representatives," Emily interrupted. "They represent singers—all types of musicians."

"Young lady, it's early to bed for you," Nanny said to Amanda.

"But Jack could come and take us in the

car!" Amanda pleaded. "Nanny, you're so special to me, Nanny. Please, please, please."

Nanny thought for a moment, stood tall, and answered, "It's all very unusual. I can't get in touch with your parents, but since you were so disappointed this morning— Just this once, perhaps. And Jack will wait for you."

"Of course! Jack is totally reliable," Amanda added, smiling. "You are such a splendid nanny."

Emily and Amanda sat together, drinking milk and eating wonderful sandwiches. Emily thought they were light as feathers! "I ate so much at your cousin's party—except for the quails' eggs—I didn't think I'd have room for anything else—ever! Your rooms are so big. And there are so many beautiful things here. Your parents must have an enormous place! At home, my mom and dad's room is right across the hall. They can hear everything I do! If I let the dog get up on my bed, my mom comes running. Are your parents right nearby, too?"

Amanda tapped her fingers on the table, even though she knew it wasn't proper. "Across the hall? My parents never seem to be nearby. In fact, they are away yet again," she answered. Then she looked intently at Emily. "I'm so grateful to you, Emily. This day had started out so horribly, and because of some kind of magic, I suppose, and now because of you, it's turned into adventure, fun, and a perfect time!"

"I was just going to say the same thing to you!" Emily turned to Amanda in astonishment. "You know, my parents promised me they'd spend this whole day with me, touring London—"

"Playing games! Talking, maybe a picnic—whatever I wanted!"

"And at the last minute, they had some stupid business appointment—"

"To fly to Scotland—"

"And they put me on this children's tour—"

"Cousin George's birthday party—"

"*And this always happens!*" they finished together.

"Parents!" Emily said, making a face.

"So it's not just me whose parents have such a very busy schedule."

"Bet your crown it isn't!"

"Come with me, please," Amanda said, motioning to Emily. "Over here."

"The mirror?"

"Yes. Look."

They studied each other.

"You sure have pretty hair," Emily said at last.

Amanda laughed. "You do, too. Beautiful. You know, I never thought my hair was pretty until I saw it on you."

"We *could* be twins, you know. Your nanny was right."

"Yes. . . ." Amanda laughed.

"I wish you could visit *me,*" Emily said. "We're only five minutes away from Manhattan, across the East River in Brooklyn Heights. Wouldn't that be fabulous? My friends would die!"

"I'd love to see the way you live."

Emily's face fell a little. "It's—different," she said.

"Of course!"

"No, I mean, really not at all like your world. Nobody waits on me—except my mother, and that's only when I'm sick in bed."

"You do everything for yourself?"

"Exactly. And I do things for my mom, too. Take out the trash, clean my room, wipe dishes . . . My mom or my baby-sitter makes dinner, not a cook. We only have *one* kitchen. Oh, and *I* walk the dog. She's a mutt."

"A life like that must allow you so much freedom!" Amanda said.

"Freedom? Well . . . I never thought of it like that."

"Emily, can you decide what you'd like to wear every day?"

Emily thought about that morning and her pink dress, then answered, "Most of the time."

"Can you draw your own bath?"

"If I wanted to take a bath. But I guess I mostly take showers."

"Can you walk to school by yourself without a person guarding you?"

"Well . . . sure!"

"I *would* love to visit you, Emily."

Amanda caught the scent of lavender in the air and turned around.

"Nanny, Emily has invited me to visit her in the United States. Isn't that lovely? She lives in New York City. I'm going to do it someday. Before I'm twelve!" Amanda added suddenly.

"Do what?" Emily and Nanny said at once.

"Come to America. To Brooklyn Heights. To visit you, Emily!"

"Nanny, we need to change our clothes to attend this concert. Let's not be late."

"How do I look in *this*?" Emily asked.

Amanda eyed Emily's black leggings and black jumper. "You look divine. We're not twins now. I'll take this hat. Does this dress make me look older?" Amanda wondered.

"Yes, you do look older and gorgeous," Emily agreed, and then laughed. "You look just like the fourteen-year-old English girl I described in my postcard."

"Jack is ready with the car, Amanda," Nanny said stiffly. She examined her charge carefully. "Are you quite sure about the hat?"

Amanda smiled. "Quite sure, Nanny. I like it with this frock."

"Very well, then, off you go. I still think I should accompany you."

"Jack will take good care of us, thank you, Nanny." Amanda touched Nanny's hand. "I am growing up, you know. I'll still need you, Nanny, but not everywhere I go, all the time."

"Yes," Nanny said, and turned away. "I hope you both enjoy yourselves. It was a pleasure to meet you, Emily Jane."

"The pleasure was mine," Emily said, remembering one of her mother's favorite expressions.

The girls kept very still in the back of the car, while Jack sat in the front with the chauffeur. Occasionally one girl would look at the other and giggle.

Suddenly Emily said, "I'll try."

160

"What?" Amanda asked. "You'll try what?"

"I'll try listening to music without feeling jealous about my parents giving their time to their work," Emily explained.

Amanda smiled. "And *I* am going to do something, too," she said, folding her hands and planting them firmly in her lap.

"And what's that?" Emily asked.

"Visit the United States. Come to New York City. Visit you and see how you live!"

"Do you think you'll really be able to?"

"I don't know yet. But if you can be a princess at a palace party and I can have a lemonade at a snack bar with a group of foreign tourists, then between us, I think we can do anything!"

"I think you're right!" Emily agreed. They shook hands firmly and grinned at each other.

"I promise that I'll behave myself when I get to meet the Mashed Potatoes! I won't sing along!" Amanda said, and then laughed at Emily's horrified expression.

"As long as *I* don't have to." Emily laughed. "I just hope my parents don't exchange me for you!"